Remembering Minidoka

A Journal from an Internment Camp

By Margaret Nevinski
Illustrated by Cynthia Samul

Acknowledgments

Grateful thanks to the Bainbridge Island Historical Museum and members of the Bainbridge Island Japanese American community.

Remembering Minidoka:
A Journal from an Internment Camp
Text © Margaret Nevinski
Illustrations copyright ©2001 The McGraw-Hill Companies, Inc.
Illustrations by Cynthia Samul

SUNSHINE™ is a trademark of The McGraw-Hill Companies Inc.

Wright Group/McGraw-Hill
19201 120th Avenue NE
Bothell, WA 98011
www.WrightGroup.com

Printed in China through Colorcraft Ltd, Hong Kong

10 9 8 7 6 5 4 3 2 1

ISBN: 0-322-04499-5
ISBN: 0-322-04595-9 (6-pack)

Contents

Foreword

On December 7, 1941, Japanese aircraft bombed Pearl Harbor, Hawaii, forcing the United States to declare war on Japan and enter World War II.

Many people worried that Japanese Americans living on the West Coast of the United States would not be loyal to America during the war.

In February 1942, President Franklin Roosevelt signed Executive Order 9066. The order said that all persons of Japanese ancestry living on the West Coast in Washington, Oregon, and California must leave their homes. Most of these people were American citizens.

Grandparents, mothers, fathers, children, and babies were moved to places called "relocation centers" or "internment camps." There were ten internment camps, mostly in desert areas in the

West. Over 100,000 people were moved to these camps.

This story takes place in Minidoka Relocation Center near Hunt, Idaho.

My house in Seattle

CHAPTER 1
Minidoka

February 12, 1944

Today is my ninth birthday! I'm celebrating by starting this journal.

My name is Lily Kato, and I'm in the third grade.

My best friend here at camp, Yuki, gave me this journal when we stood in line at the mess hall for breakfast this morning. Yuki's full name is Yukiko, but everyone calls her Yuki.

The lines are so long here at camp that Yuki couldn't wait until we got our food and sat down. She is the most impatient person I know. She is also the smartest. Especially in math, which I hate. But I love to write, so she gave me the perfect present.

Guess what? Yuki used to live in Seattle, too! We made a promise today to

My best friend, Yuki, and me

be sisters forever. Since neither of us has a real sister, I know we will never break our promise. Ever.

I have one brother, Ben, who is thirteen. He plays first base on our block's baseball team here at Minidoka.

Minidoka is the camp where we have lived for a year and a half. Mama says we must always remember our house back in Seattle. We lived there until the Japanese bombed Pearl Harbor. That day changed our lives forever.

Our family had nothing to do with the bombing, but we had to move to Minidoka just because we are Japanese Americans. Papa says it's not fair. Papa is always right. He told the government men that the United States is also at war with Germany, but our German American neighbors, the Schmidts, were not sent away to a camp.

Mama and Papa are Issei, which means they were born in Japan and then moved to America. The government will not let them become American citizens even though they want to. Ben and I are Nisei, which means our parents were born in Japan and we were born in America. How can we be dangerous? We have never even been to Japan!

We left Seattle on April 28, 1942. We could take only what we could carry. I was seven, and Mama said I could choose one toy. I decided to bring Spotty, my stuffed giraffe.

First a bus took us to Camp Harmony, near Seattle. We stayed at Camp Harmony until August when we moved here to Minidoka. Soldiers put us on the train, and I was scared. I could tell Ben was scared, too. We thought we had done something wrong. The train took us

through the mountains and the desert until we arrived at Minidoka.

Papa says that Japanese Americans must prove we are loyal to the United States. He says that we will see justice at the end of the war. I hope so. Papa's never been wrong before.

February 20, 1944

Yuki says I should write down all the important things I may forget later. When Yuki says that, I know she is talking about numbers. So here they are: Minidoka is like a small city. Each family is given a number. My family's number is 13517. We live in Block 15, Barrack 5, Apartment D. Our apartment has one room for four people. The room is 16 feet by 20 feet. There are about 8,000 people at Minidoka and almost 500 barracks in all. There. Are you happy, Yuki?

March 15, 1944

Tonight after supper at the mess hall, Aunt Kiku came to visit. She is Mama's younger sister and our favorite aunt. She lives in Barrack 8 with three other single women.

Sometimes Mama feels sad about living here at Minidoka. She misses her garden and the birds and the squirrels. There are no animals here. Mrs. Sako, the grumpy lady next door, had to give away her pet collie, Minnie.

Aunt Kiku always cheers Mama up. Sometimes she brings us a treat from the canteen where she works as a clerk. Tonight, Aunt Kiku gave us each a candy bar. The chocolate was soft, and soon we had chocolate all over our hands and faces. Mama smiled and shook her head before looking for a rag.

It is impossible to keep clean here. Our only water comes from the laundry, and it is Ben's job to bring water to our apartment every day. But often he is out with his friends. He usually eats with them, too.

Mama shakes her head when she talks about Ben, but this time there is no smile. It upsets her that Ben spends more time with his friends than he does at home. Papa shrugs and says, "What can you expect? This isn't a real home."

Mama still has that sad look on her face. Sometimes even Aunt Kiku can't make it go away.

CHAPTER 2
Dust Storm

May 17, 1944

Today was a school day. Our school meets in a barrack. When we said the Pledge of Allegiance, I raised my voice when we came to the last words: "with liberty and justice for all."

Yuki leaned over and giggled. "The guards can hear you all the way over in the watchtowers," she whispered.

I don't care. I think there should be justice for everybody.

Our teacher, Miss Mori, told us we were going to write stories. A few kids (like Yuki) groaned, but not me. I love to make up stories. In my stories no one lives in a camp. Everyone lives in a beautiful house with lots of dogs and cats and a big grassy yard. There is no grass here, only acres of sand and sagebrush.

Miss Mori is still a college student. She looks like a glamorous movie star with long, shiny hair.

Miss Mori complains that we don't have enough books or pens or paper. Sometimes she gets a package of supplies

from white friends outside the camp. That's what happened today. She received a box of beautiful clean paper. We each got one piece.

I had just begun my story when another teacher rushed into our room. She had a worried look on her face. She told Miss Mori that the wind was starting.

We all knew what that meant. A dust storm! I was so busy writing that I didn't notice the dust coming through the cracks in the wall. Miss Mori and the other teacher talked about what to do. Finally they decided to send us home to our barracks. They were afraid the wind would get worse.

They sent us home in pairs. Miss Mori told us to stay together no matter what. I hoped it wouldn't rain. When it rains at Minidoka, the roads turn into slippery, brown mud.

Yuki and I held hands and set out for Block 15. The wind hit us as soon as we stepped out the door. Swirling dust was everywhere. We kept our eyes on the dirt road. Soon dust covered us from head to toe. I could feel dirt in my teeth and hair and eyes.

When Yuki and I got home, we had trouble opening the door. The wind kept

knocking it closed. Mama came to our rescue. She helped us inside and hugged us both tight. Yuki and I looked like dust snowmen. We started to laugh and finally Mama joined in. She was so happy I was home.

Mama walked Yuki home. Now she is worried about Papa and Ben. It's five o'clock, and they are not here yet. Papa is at a meeting. He goes to a lot of meetings.

Later. I'm writing this in bed. The sheets are gritty with sand. Spotty, my giraffe, has more spots than ever.

Papa found Ben with his friends at the canteen. Aunt Kiku was there, too. So we are all safe. I wish Aunt Kiku would bring us another candy bar. We missed dinner at the mess hall because of the dust storm.

Outside, we can still hear the wind blowing. Sand sifts through the cracks and covers Mama's clean floor. Even so, she and Papa express thanks that we are all okay.

CHAPTER 3
Sad News

August 2, 1944

Today when I came home from art class, Mama sat with Mrs. Sako in our apartment. She was crying. Mama told me to go to Yuki's. Before I left, I heard Mrs. Sako sobbing, "Why him? Why him?"

Later I found out what happened. Mrs. Sako's only son, Ronald, was killed in the war. He was in Italy.

Papa told us that when the war began, the United States government didn't allow Japanese American men to fight.

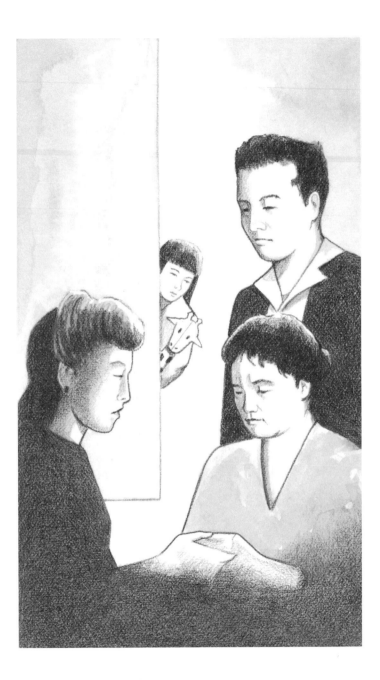

Then, last year, President Roosevelt said they could join the army. The army formed a special unit of only Nisei men.

Ronald was nineteen. Mama said that Ronald was killed while saving another man's life.

Mrs. Sako is alone now. Her husband died before the war. Ronald didn't have to go to war, but he wanted to prove that he was loyal to the United States.

"Some proof," I heard Papa grumble. Mama told him to hush. She doesn't like to hear him talk that way.

"Kodomo no tame ni," she said. I don't always understand when Mama and Papa speak Japanese, but I know what that means. It means, "For the sake of the children."

Now I feel bad that I said Mrs. Sako was grumpy. She was just worried about her son.

August 7, 1944

Today I picked some daisies for Mrs. Sako. Mama wanted a flower garden, so she planted some flowers at the end of our barrack. She waters the plants every

day, but sometimes they die from the heat. Today at noon it was over one hundred degrees.

Ben was home, and he and I went next door. Mrs. Sako said thank you, but her eyes were dry and glassy. When we got home, Mama looked at Ben a long time. Then she said, "I hope this war is over before you turn eighteen."

Luckily, Aunt Kiku arrived then. She brought Frank Ito, the man she met in a night class. We call him Frank-san. He is more serious than Aunt Kiku, but he loves to make her laugh.

Whenever Aunt Kiku is here, we can joke and pretend that there is no war. But tonight we all had trouble pretending. We could hear Mrs. Sako crying through the thin walls. Mama said, *"Shikata ga nai,"* which means, "It cannot be helped. It just has to be." She says that a lot lately.

I asked Frank-san whether he would have to go to the war. He told us that he tried to enlist last year, but his eyesight is too bad for him to join the army. Frank-san wears thick glasses that help him see when he types. He writes news and stories for our camp newspaper, *The Minidoka Irrigator*.

Frank-san told me that someday he will take me to the newspaper office and let me use his typewriter—just like a real writer.

After a while Mama took a cup of tea to Mrs. Sako. Mama came back and said that our neighbor had to cry alone. I wish Mrs. Sako still had her collie, Minnie.

CHAPTER 4

A Trip Outside Camp

October 11, 1944

An exciting day! Our class went on a field trip to Twin Falls. That's a big town near Minidoka. Everyone was happy as we loaded the bus. The sky was bright blue and for once the dust wasn't swirling. Even the guard smiled at us from his watchtower. I smiled back because Mama taught us to be polite to strangers.

We have a new teacher for fourth grade, Mrs. Olson. She doesn't look like a movie star. She is a white lady who used to teach before her children grew up. Miss Mori got permission to go back to college. She couldn't return to her school in Seattle, though. Instead, she went to a college in New York City.

Papa told us that Japanese Americans cannot return to their homes and schools on the West Coast yet. The government still thinks we are dangerous.

When Miss Mori told us she was going to New York City, I tried to imagine the tall buildings and the Statue of Liberty. I decided I will write a story about Miss Mori and her adventures.

Back to the bus. Yuki and I crowded together at the window so we could both see. We were disappointed at first. Sagebrush was everywhere. Just like at

Minidoka. Finally we came to a river and saw some trees with bright orange and yellow leaves. We saw a field where Japanese American men were working. Sometimes Papa gets permission to pick sugar beets to earn money, but he wasn't in the field today, so I didn't wave.

The bus arrived at Twin Falls. Yuki's and my eyes popped open. We saw cars, stores, and white people shopping just like it was an ordinary day. For them, it was an ordinary day, I guess. For us, it was *extraordinary*. That's a word Miss Mori taught us last year.

October 12, 1944

It's the next day. I had to quit writing yesterday because Mama sent me for water. I told her that was Ben's job, but as usual, Ben was playing baseball with his friends. Sometimes it's not fair being a girl. I grumbled all the way to the laundry until I remembered that Mrs. Sako didn't have anyone to get water for her. So I went back and got her bucket, too.

On the way to the laundry, I stopped at the latrine. Aunt Kiku was there. Mama would say that I shouldn't write about things like latrines in a journal, but Yuki would say that it's important to remember everything. I think Yuki is right.

The latrine is a big bathroom that everyone in our block shares. At first that was hard to get used to. Aunt Kiku said, "Think of it this way—you don't have to wait until school to see your friends." Aunt Kiku always sees the bright side.

I was glad when I saw her at the latrine. I wanted to ask her about something I saw yesterday in Twin Falls. We went to a school to sing for the students there. Mrs. Olson had taught us several songs for the program. We sang "This Land Is Your Land" and "You Are My Sunshine" and "Red River Valley," which is a very sad song. All the students and teachers at the school were white. After the program, they clapped loudly and we had lemonade and cookies together.

But when we walked back to the bus, I saw a store with a sign in the window. The sign said, "Japs Go Home!" I felt my face go red. I was too ashamed to say anything, even to Yuki. Why do some people think we are the enemy?

That's what I asked Aunt Kiku. For once she looked serious. "Lily-chan," she said. (That's what my family calls me sometimes.) "Some people hate, and it is out of ignorance. They are worried about their sons fighting the Japanese."

"But I'm not Japanese. I'm American. I was born in Seattle."

"I know that," she said. "But they don't. They see only your face. To them, your face is Japanese, not American."

Now I am confused. Am I Japanese or American? Or both?

I walked back to our barrack with the buckets of water. All around me I saw Japanese faces. I know Mama and Papa love their homeland, Japan. They are worried about our relatives there and can't write letters to them.

But Mama and Papa love America, too. Why can't people love two countries?

If wars make people hate, I don't see why we fight them.

CHAPTER 5
A Christmas Wedding

December 9, 1944

Good news! Aunt Kiku is getting married!
She and Frank-san made the announce-
ment while Mama made tea. It was a
special occasion, so Mama brought out
the chocolates that the Schmidts sent for
her birthday.

Aunt Kiku said that if she and Frank-
san get married on Christmas Eve Day,
they will never forget their anniversary.
Guess what? I get to be the flower girl!

Her roommate, Sue, will be a bridesmaid.

Ben said, "I don't have to be a flower boy, do I?" Everyone laughed. Then we asked Frank-san if we can call him Uncle Frank now.

"Sure," he said, and he didn't do anything dumb like pat my head. I think Uncle Frank will be a very good uncle.

December 20, 1944

Mama has been busy sewing my dress. She ordered the material from a catalog. The dress is white with tiny red dots. When I tried it on, Ben said I looked like I had the measles.

I made a face, but Mama told me not to pay attention. "Big brothers are supposed to say things like that," she said. She should know. She has a big brother, our Uncle Mitsu. We have never met him. He lives in Hiroshima, Japan.

December 24, 1944

Today was Aunt Kiku's wedding day! I am writing this quickly, before I go to sleep, so I will remember every single thing. Tomorrow morning when I wake up, it will be Christmas.

Aunt Kiku looked beautiful. Her face was very pale. Her friends at the canteen gave her a big bouquet of flowers. I got to walk up the aisle of the church (which is in a barrack), and I didn't even trip.

After the wedding, everyone came to our apartment for a party. All the guests brought a special food. Someone had oranges, which we have not eaten in a long time.

I didn't think so many people could fit into our small room. Even Mrs. Sako was there. Mama handed her a cup of tea and Mrs. Sako smiled. Later Mama told Papa, "It's a start." I am very glad Uncle Frank has bad eyesight and can't join the army. I wouldn't want Aunt Kiku to be sad like Mrs. Sako.

Before everyone left, Mama sang a song in Japanese. It was a song she remembered from when she was a girl in Japan. I couldn't make out all the words, but it was about a bride and cherry blossoms. Some older people had tears in their eyes. I think they were remembering when they were young.

Aunt Kiku is a married woman now.
I hope she doesn't change too much.

Aunt Kiku's wedding

December 25, 1944

Snow! Papa woke us up by sprinkling snowflakes on our faces. After Ben and I screamed, we ran outside in our pajamas. It was cold: zero degrees. Minidoka looked like a fairyland.

Somehow Mama found a tiny Christmas tree. She said she wants the holiday to be the way it was in Seattle with a tree and lights and presents. I was afraid to tell Mama that I have forgotten about Christmas in Seattle. All I remember is going downtown to visit Santa Claus and seeing toys in all the department store windows.

Papa thinks we will be home next Christmas. I'm going to make that my Christmas wish.

Mama opened the package we received from the Schmidts. The smell of fresh evergreen bows filled the room and made Mama's eyes tear up. I didn't want her to cry, so I gave her my gift next. In art class I made a watercolor painting of our house in Seattle, at least how I remembered it. Uncle Frank helped me frame it. But my picture made Mama's eyes tear up even more.

Luckily, Yuki came over then. I gave her a wooden ruler Papa helped me make. She can use it for arithmetic. Yuki gave me a bright red pencil, which is good. I'm down to a stub with this one.

We had Christmas dinner at the mess hall, and for once we didn't have to stand in line. We all sat at a big table. They brought us turkey and potatoes and string beans (canned) and pumpkin pie. I sat with Mama, Papa, Ben, Aunt Kiku, Uncle Frank, Mrs. Sako, Yuki, and Yuki's parents. Aunt Kiku and Uncle Frank kept holding hands under the table.

After we ate, everyone sang "Silent Night." When we sang the last word, "peace," it was quiet in the mess hall. It was the quietest quiet I have ever heard.

CHAPTER 6
Going Home!

February 12, 1945

Papa got news today! The government said that Japanese Americans can return to their homes in Washington, Oregon, and California. I thought Mama would cry, but instead she and Aunt Kiku jumped up and down. Imagine Mama jumping! Just like me and Yuki.

I told Yuki that I was happy we'd be going home soon, but I was scared, too.

Yuki nodded. We're not sure where home is anymore. When we go back to Seattle, we hope we'll be in the same school.

My family rented out our house when we left, and we don't know if we can go back there. Mama doesn't care. *"Shikata ga nai,"* she says. She just wants our family back together in a regular house with a garden and flowers and squirrels.

Papa is trying to get his old job back. He has been writing letters. Even though we are going home, Papa reminded us that we are still at war with Japan. I remembered the sign I saw: "Japs Go Home!" Will that happen to us when we return to Seattle?

In all the excitement, I almost forgot that today is my tenth birthday!

Happy Birthday to me!

March 15, 1945

Today Ben played in a baseball game. We all went to the game, even Mrs. Sako. She brought a blanket for sitting on the hard bleachers. Ben hit a single in the ninth inning that brought a runner home. Everyone cheered, and I felt proud that Ben was my brother.

Ben—March 15, 1945

Yesterday Ben told me that he is scared to leave Minidoka, too. He'll miss his teammates. We're worried about how we will be accepted at school.

Papa says we will go home within a month. His boss offered him his old job back. We have to find a new place to live, though. Mama says we will share a house with Aunt Kiku and Uncle Frank at first.

Late last night Aunt Kiku came over. I was almost asleep, but I heard her whispering to Mama. I got up and sat in Mama's lap even though I'm too big for that now. I brought Spotty, my giraffe.

Aunt Kiku said, "May I tell her?"

"What?" I asked sleepily. Aunt Kiku told me that she and Uncle Frank are expecting a baby. I flung my arms around her, and she laughed. Mama started to cry, but this time I knew it was from happiness.

The baby will be born in the fall. I hope it will be a girl. We'll be back home in Seattle then. When the baby is my age, I'll tell her about growing up in Minidoka. And I'll let her read my journal. She'll find out all about Yuki and Mrs. Sako and Miss Mori, who went to New York City.

Now I have my own story to tell. It's a story I always want to remember.

Afterword

The United States dropped atomic bombs on Hiroshima and Nagasaki, Japan, in August 1945, ending the war with Japan.

Beginning in early 1945, Japanese Americans were allowed to return to their homes in Washington, Oregon, and California. Many, however, moved to different cities where they could find houses and jobs. Some found prejudice when they returned. Others were welcomed home.

In 1976, on the thirty-fourth anniversary of Executive Order 9066, President Gerald Ford said that what the United States government had done was wrong. In 1988, President Ronald Reagan signed the Civil Liberties Act. This act officially acknowledged that, in the words of Gerald Ford, "We now know what we should have known then...Japanese Americans were and are loyal Americans."